Matthew Likes to Read

by Jan Grainger

pictures by Lesley Moyes

Ready to Read

Learning Media
Wellington

Matthew likes to read.

He reads all sorts of things.

He reads all the words he can see.

Matthew reads the newspaper.

"A storm hit Southland today."

He reads the weather.

"Today was wet and cold.

Tomorrow will be fine."

3

STOP

NO RIGHT TURN

GIVE WAY

Wellingto

4

He reads signs by the road.
"Wellington 6 kilometres."
"No right turn."
"Give way."
"Stop."

5

6

He reads the directions
on the soup packets.
"Add water. Stir well.
Cook for five minutes.
Serves four."

Matthew reads train tickets.
"One trip between
Wellington and Lower Hutt."

He reads labels in shops.

"Please do not touch."

"←Toys."

"Lifts↑↓."

"Sale now on."

9

Matthew and Mum
have come to the supermarket.
"Oh, dear," says Mum.
"I have lost my shopping list."

"That's all right," says Matthew.
"I read that, too.
Butter, sugar, flour, eggs,
and ice cream."

11